ADVENTURES IN FRONTIER AMERICA

Indiana Days

Life in a Frontier Town

by Catherine E. Chambers
illustrated by John Lawn

Troll

Kristi Birkett was furious.

"I don't want to be sent away to Indiana! I want to stay here in Iowa Territory with you and Mama and the little ones. I don't need fancy manners here on the prairie!"

Pa took his pipe out of his mouth. "No use arguing," he said mildly. "Your Ma's mind is made up, and I agree. It's not fitting—your growing up wild with no book learning."

"I don't care about those things!"

"You should. Your Grandma Birkett was smart as a whip, like you. She taught all her young ones to read and write. Only I didn't pay attention. That's why you've already outgrown all I could teach you. Your Ma's plenty smart, too, only in the old country she didn't have a chance to go to school. You do. So make the most of it."

3

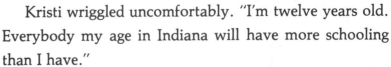

Kristi wriggled uncomfortably. "I'm twelve years old. Everybody my age in Indiana will have more schooling than I have."

"Then I count on you to catch up fast." Pa's face frowned, but his eyes were twinkling. "Might as well accept it, Kristi. Only a stupid critter keeps on struggling once it knows it's roped. And I've already written your Aunt Charity and Uncle Dan Craig to expect you."

Kristi didn't want to leave her family. She loved living in the sod house, which was so cozy warm when winds howled outside. She was proud of being a "soddie." She didn't want to be teased about it by boys and girls who lived in wooden houses.

Her brother Carl got into fights with the boys from town who jeered at him because he was a "soddie." He teased Kristi that the same thing would happen to her. Then Pa heard him and gave him a talking-to, and that stopped that.

4

Kristi was scared, but she'd have died rather than admit it. She helped Ma with weaving and sewing new clothes for her trip. She was going to stay with the Craigs for a whole year, until June 1842.

"You've grown so fast, hardly any of your old things will do." Mama's eyes were proud but sad. "By the time you come home you'll be a real young lady."

Kristi didn't like the sound of that. But she loved her new clothes, made from the wool of their own sheep. There was a heavy shawl in a plaid pattern Mama had learned in the old country. There were skirts and tops of linsey-woolsey, a material made of linen and wool. And there were dresses of calico for which Mama had bartered at the trading station. In the evenings, Kristi helped Mama with

6

tucking and gathering, hemming and embroidering.
Mama even showed Kristi how to trim cuffs and collars
with Norwegian stitchery. Kristi had never had trimmed
clothes before. She began to feel proud of being so grown-
up. She and her mother worked by candlelight until their
eyes were strained.

At last, the painted chest that had come with Mama from Norway was filled. One May dawn, Pa went to hitch the big white horses to the wagon. All Kristi's younger sisters and brothers lined up by the door to say good-bye.

Carl pulled Kristi out into the cold crisp dawn. "I didn't mean to make it hard on you with my teasing. Here." He pressed something into her hand.

"Carl, that's the knife Pa gave you for Christmas!"

"Take it. It'll remind you you're a soddie, and soddies can take care of themselves." He ran off before she could embarrass him with a hug.

Mama came out, holding her old blue shawl tightly around her. Her crown of braids gleamed gold in the early light. "Remember you're a Birkett, and a Viking, so you don't ever have to be afraid." She pinned something to Kristi's collar.

"Mama, your *solje*." A *solje* was the silver brooch passed down in Norwegian families from mother to daughter. In the old country it often represented all the family's wealth.

"It's time you had it," Mama said. She kissed Kristi and held her close until Pa came round with the wagon.

Pa and Kristi rode across the endless prairie as the pale gray light turned to pink, and pink to rose, and rose to yellow. Pa didn't talk much. He never did. Kristi felt good just sitting next to him.

At the trading post they waited in silence for the stage. This was a wagon just like Pa's, only bigger. It had the same backless boards for seats. Their neighbor Mrs. Olesen was on the stage, going to visit her married daughter. Pa asked her to look after Kristi till she reached the town where she would take a train.

Journeys through the wide spaces of America took several days. At night everybody had to get off the stage and find lodging. Although some towns had hotels or inns, only men and some traveling couples stayed in them. Women traveling alone stayed at boarding houses, so that is what Kristi and Mrs. Olesen planned to do.

Riding on the stage for hours made Kristi stiff. But she found the train ride exciting. The train snuffed and snorted like a buffalo. The bright bell by the smokestack rang continually. Smoke belched from the firebox. A cow-catcher jutted out in front to push stubborn animals off the

tracks. The engineer sounded a shrill whistle whenever he came near stops or crossings. Inside the train were rows of seats and a center aisle.

When the train pulled into an Illinois town at dusk, a pleasant middle-aged clergyman came up to Kristi. "How do you do, my dear? I'm the Reverend Morris. This is my daughter Sarah, who went to school with your Cousin Elizabeth." This was how unescorted young women and children were looked after when traveling, by relatives and friends and friends-of-friends.

A wooden walk ran from the railroad station past a saloon, a general store, and a sheriff's office. Split logs served as guard rails and as a place to hitch horses. The church was low and square, made of weathered boards. The house where the Morrises lived was painted white. The curtains were of store-bought cloth. Kristi was very tired and didn't talk much, not even when she was tucked in under the woven coverlet with Sarah Morris. She wondered if the Morrises had brought the maple four-poster bed with them from the East. She wondered if her cousins' house would be this splendid, and if the folks in Indiana would laugh at her.

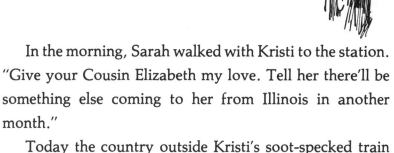

In the morning, Sarah walked with Kristi to the station. "Give your Cousin Elizabeth my love. Tell her there'll be something else coming to her from Illinois in another month."

Today the country outside Kristi's soot-specked train window was very different. No more prairies now, but rolling farmland. Here and there in the forest, dogwood trees were in bloom. The air was like summer. Kristi folded her new shawl carefully. She was glad she was wearing Mama's *solje* and the heavy leather shoes that pinched her with their newness.

The train's shrill whistle blew.

She had arrived in Indiana. The town where she was to meet her uncle was so big—it had not only a saloon and a general store, but a two-story white building marked HOTEL. The church was white, with a steeple. The feed-and-grain store was painted a cheerful yellow. There were wagons rolling down the street, and ladies walking with shopping baskets on their arms. A brown-and-white dog wriggled happily in the dust.

The train conductor grandly handed her down.

A wagon was waiting, a blue wagon with two gray horses. The man at the reins wore a broad-brimmed hat and had dashing side-whiskers, not a beard like Pa's. He smiled at Kristi, but it was the dark-haired youth next to him that she noticed. He was the very image of her brother Carl!

"So this is my Iowa niece! We're very glad to see you. I'm your Uncle Dan, and this is your Cousin Paul."

They loaded Kristi's trunk, helped her up, and clattered out into open country. Kristi couldn't believe the weather was already so warm in May. Around the tidy homesteads, flowers were blooming. Willow trees dropped lacy fingers to the river.

Kristi found her voice. "Is this the Ohio River? Pa told me how you and Aunt Charity traveled it by flatboat."

"It's the Wabash," Paul said. He gave her a look that said, *Isn't that just like a girl?* Kristi pressed her lips together tightly.

They rode for an hour through open homestead country. Then the horses turned through a gateway in a

14

picket fence. There was a big maple tree with a swing in the
side yard. And there was a strange tree with beautiful
flowers on it. Kristi looked at Paul, and, in a lordly voice,
he said, "That's a shadblow tree."

The house was of smooth white clapboards. On the porch a welcoming party stood. There was a sweet-faced woman with dark hair who looked like Pa, and a pretty young woman. There were two little boys and a laughing little girl. Aunt Charity and Cousin Elizabeth wore filmy dresses that spread over wide petticoats like full-blown flowers. Kristi was conscious of her heavy shoes and the skimpy skirt of her own home-woven dress. She thought she saw pity in Cousin Elizabeth's dark eyes, and her chin lifted. Only the shaggy gray-and-white dog, bouncing up to lick her, seemed to welcome her with uncritical delight.

I'm never going to feel at home here, Kristi thought.

The house had furniture unlike any Kristi had seen before. In the "front room," kept for important occasions and special guests, were lace curtains and a looking glass above the mantel. Cousin Elizabeth took Kristi upstairs. "Mama and Papa's room is in front," she said as they passed the door. "Ours is next, and Paul's and the children's rooms are in the back." So many bedrooms! At home, Pa and Mama slept downstairs, and all the children shared the loft together. Elizabeth's bed had a ruffle around the sides to keep out drafts, and a beautiful coverlet of fabric circles. Elizabeth saw Kristi looking at it. "I'll teach you to make one, if you like. Sarah Morris showed me how, when we were at school."

17

Kristi remembered the message Sarah had sent. She wondered why Cousin Elizabeth blushed when she heard it.

They ate supper in a room meant just for eating. In the evening, the family sat in a sitting room, not the kitchen. Kristi felt as if Indiana was a world as strange and different as Mama's Norway.

School felt strange, too. The schoolhouse stood in a flowery meadow. Kristi felt ashamed to admit she had only worked up through the Fourth Reader so far. She mumbled when she said that, and Miss Alcock, the teacher, asked her to speak up. Cousin Paul turned red, over where he sat on the boys' benches. When Kristi made a mistake in arithmetic, he turned redder still. He was ashamed of her! Kristi was mad at him, and even madder at herself. When Miss Alcock rang the lunch bell, she took her basket and went off by herself.

"Fine, Ma'am," Kristi murmured when Aunt Charity asked her how the day had gone. In the weeks that followed she kept on saying "Fine." She didn't even say that much unless she was asked. She was lonesome for the

prairies, for Pa and Mama, and for her little brothers and sisters, who used to snuggle up to her while she told them stories.

One day Kristi won the spelling match in school. Miss Alcock asked her to stay after the others were dismissed. She offered to help Kristi with extra work. "You are a very bright girl, Kristi. The only reason you didn't go beyond Fourth Reader was because no one gave you anything more difficult to try. I can loan you Shakespeare and *Pilgrim's Progress.* Your aunt and uncle own books, too. If you study hard, you could go on to boarding school like Elizabeth did."

Kristi knew there were many private schools for young women now, just as there were for young men. She certainly didn't want to go to one! But she loved the books Miss Alcock loaned her. The arithmetic problems were like the puzzle games Pa used to dream up for her and Carl on winter nights.

When June came, she had the highest grades in school, just ahead of her Cousin Paul.

"You must have a new dress for Closing Exercises," Aunt Charity said warmly. Kristi thought she ought to wear the blue-checked one Mama had worked on so carefully. But she wanted the Craigs to be proud of her when she rose to accept her prize. Aunt Charity made her a white dress, its three flounces edged with printed borders just like a picture in *Godey's Lady's Book*, the ladies' magazine that Aunt Charity and Cousin Elizabeth liked to read. She wore the collar and cuffs Mama had embroidered and Mama's *solje.*

Everyone came to Closing Excercises, not just the students and their parents. The mayor was there and the doctor and the minister. The minister's wife "set the tune," or hummed each line of music before it was sung, and the crowd sang a hymn. The president of the school board gave out perfect-attendance certificates. He gave diplomas to the three graduating students. For her high marks, he gave Kristi a volume of Shakespeare, bound in brown leather. Then the grownups had a spelling bee. Kristi found this great fun. She was as proud as the others when Aunt Charity won. But she still hadn't made any friends here. She still didn't feel that she belonged.

Aunt Charity and Uncle Dan worried over her. Once she heard them discussing her with Paul and Elizabeth. "Maybe she's just not used to people," Uncle Dan said. "The old pioneer spirit. She likes to keep to herself."

"I think she's stuck-up," Paul snorted. "She acts like she's too good for the rest of us. Especially since she won that prize!" Kristi blinked at that. Surely it was the other way around!

Anyway, I have two friends, she thought fiercely. Shep the dog loved her. And Rebecca, her littlest cousin, cuddled close for stories just as the little ones did at home.

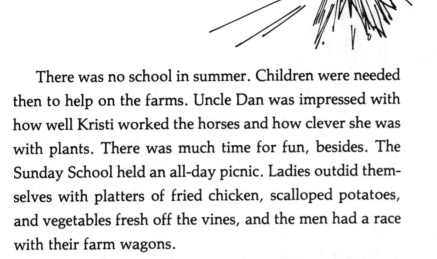

There was no school in summer. Children were needed then to help on the farms. Uncle Dan was impressed with how well Kristi worked the horses and how clever she was with plants. There was much time for fun, besides. The Sunday School held an all-day picnic. Ladies outdid themselves with platters of fried chicken, scalloped potatoes, and vegetables fresh off the vines, and the men had a race with their farm wagons.

On the Fourth of July, the Craigs were up at dawn. A great celebration was being held in town. Flags were flying, small boys were shooting off firecrackers, and dogs were running everywhere and barking. A platform in front of the hotel was hung with banners. Several men made speeches—the mayor, the president of the school board, and a tall gaunt man with a kind smile. "That's Abe Lincoln from over in Illinois," Uncle Dan whispered. "He's a well-liked speaker and politician in these parts."

Everyone sang patriotic songs. Cousin Elizabeth sang a solo. When she was finished, a handsome stranger stepped forward and handed her a bouquet. Cousin Elizabeth turned white, then pink, and her eyes shone like stars.

23

The young man was Samuel Morris, Sarah's brother. "He's silly over Elizabeth," Paul muttered. So that was what Sarah had meant by her mysterious message!

Mr. Morris asked Uncle Dan's permission to propose to Elizabeth, and Elizabeth accepted his proposal. This brought more excitement. There was much to be done before a wedding next spring. Mr. Morris bought some uncleared farmland from the government. Men and boys from nearby homesteads helped him cut down trees and clear away brush. Aunt Charity and Uncle Dan asked the cabinetmaker to make a set of front-room furniture as their wedding gift.

In August, Sarah came to visit, bringing silk scraps for a wedding quilt. Aunt Charity held a quilting party to which all the ladies came. They sat in the front room around the quilting frame. Later they went to the dining room. There were so many pies and cakes that they wouldn't all fit on the table.

Another evening a party was given to honor the young couple. A fiddler played for reels and circle dances. Aunt Charity played songs on a small organ called a melodeon. Wearing their nightclothes, the younger children peeked through the stair rails. Paul and Kristi were considered grown-up enough to attend the party. Kristi heard Uncle Dan tell Paul to ask her to dance. She heard Aunt Charity's troubled, "We don't want to embarrass the child. Suppose she doesn't know how?"

Kristi's ears got red. "I can do a jig," she said loudly. The fiddler heard her and struck up a familiar tune. Kristi was stuck. She glared at Paul, daring him. To her astonishment Paul got up with a swagger. Everybody stood round in a circle and clapped as they danced the jig. After that she wasn't scared of Paul anymore.

The frame of Cousin Elizabeth's future home had to be raised before cold weather set in. Mr. Morris took a room at Widow Bradley's boarding house. He got work as a clerk in Squire Soames's law office. Every free moment he was out working on the house. Paul and Uncle Dan worked with him when they could. Kristi helped, too. She straightened bent nails for them, the way Pa had taught her.

The house-raising was held right after harvest. All the neighbors came in wagons, bringing tools. In one day, the clapboard outer walls were built, raised, and fastened to the framework. Again, there was a picnic and dancing. All the women had brought pots and baskets of food for a "pot luck" feast.

Kristi wandered off when the dancing began. She didn't want to make a spectacle of herself again. She sat down on a log and watched the twilight gather behind the shadblow trees. Back in Iowa, frost was already casting chill upon the prairie. Her hand slipped into her pocket and fingered the knife she had brought to help with the work. What had Carl told her? Soddies could take care of themselves.

26

Suddenly, she heard somebody crying. It was Rebecca.

Kristi started to run across the fields, down into the hollow by the river bank. She saw Paul against the twilight on the next rise. He was running, too.

Rebecca was on a rock at the water's edge. She was wet. She had been playing where she oughtn't. Kristi ran forward, then stopped abruptly, shocked by a rattling noise.

Rattler. There was a big, old rattlesnake hissing at Rebecca, sticking out its tongue. Rebecca must have disturbed the snake's sleep.

The snake was so near her. Paul was so far away.

Swiftly, silent as a shadow, Kristi crept up on the rattler. Carl had taught her how when they were playing Indians. She would only have one chance. If she missed, *somebody* would get bitten. If she didn't try, Rebecca surely would.

With her left hand, she made a swift gesture for silence. Rebecca saw and obeyed. Kristi's right hand stole into her pocket. Then her hand stole out, holding tight to Carl's prized knife. She threw herself forward, and the knife flashed.

The rattler's hiss was cut short. Its head was off. The severed body, with its rattles, thrashed and lay still.

Kristi's legs went weak. She sat down. Rebecca ran over and buried herself in Kristi's lap.

Paul came running up. He stopped dead when he saw what lay before them. When he found his voice, it was shaking. "You—you sure can do pretty well, for a girl."

"*For a girl?*" Kristi's voice dared him.

"For anybody," Paul said awkwardly. His face split into a grin. "This family's got plenty to be proud of, doesn't it?"

"I guess we do learn some things out on the prairie, don't we?" Kristi beamed.

After that night, a lot of things seemed different. In school she no longer ate lunch alone. When the family went to a husking bee at another farm, she didn't hide against the barn wall. She competed with other young folks to see who was fastest at husking an ear of corn.

Christmas came, bringing a box of gifts from Kristi's family. Her eyes filled with tears when she saw the fleecy shawl Mama had knitted for her, and the handsome design on the leather bookmark Carl had made. She missed her family very much. *But Indiana's home, too, now,* she thought. The light from the oil lamp fell softly on Rebecca sleepily rocking her Christmas doll, on Elizabeth's dark head bent over needlework, on Paul sitting by the fire reading.

Mr. Morris gave Elizabeth a gold ring with a little emerald in it. They were going to be married in June.

"And Kristi shall be my maid of honor," Elizabeth said, smiling at her.

The wedding was held in the garden by the grape arbor, and the shadblows were in bloom. Elizabeth wore pale dove gray and a lace-covered bonnet with blue silk ribbons. Aunt Charity helped Kristi put her hair up. "To match Miss Sarah. I hope your mother won't think I've let you grow up too fast," Aunt Charity said.

The men wore Sunday coats, their best high collars, and silk ties. Paul had a dress coat, too, his first. He and Kristi would be graduating from school in another week.

After the wedding ceremony, there was a party in the garden. There was fruit shrub—a drink of raspberries and vinegar and spring water—and cakes and pies. The fiddler played, and everybody danced to some of the old favorite songs. Then Aunt Charity played the latest new songs on the melodeon.

I'm graduating, Kristi thought. *I have my hair up and a beautiful gown, just like Cousin Elizabeth. Maybe I'll be first in the class. Maybe Paul will. It really doesn't matter, because we're all family. In a few weeks I'll be going home to the Territory. I'll see Pa and Mama and the rest of the family. But I have family here, too, and friends. I always will have. I wonder when I'll see them again. I wonder if I could start a school in a sod house back home. Miss Alcock would help me get some books. I wonder if Paul will come visit us once harvest's in, like he says he will.*

Kristi smiled in the lantern-lit darkness as she and Paul danced by the Wabash shore.

Index

*(Page numbers that appear in **boldface** type refer to illustrations.)*

This edition published in 2003.

Printed in Canada

10 9 8 7 6 5 4 3 2

Cover art by Robert F. Goetzl.

Library of Congress Cataloging-in-Publication Data

Chambers, Catherine E.
    Indiana days.

    (Adventures in frontier America)
    Summary: In the 1840's twelve-year-old Kristi travels
from her family's sod house on the Iowa prairie to an
Indiana town to stay with relatives and get an education.
    [1. Frontier and pioneer life—Indiana—Fiction.
2. Indiana—History—Fiction]   I. Lawn, John, ill.
II. Title.   III. Series: Chambers, Catherine E.
Adventures in frontier America.
PZ7.C3558In   1984   [Fic]   83-18283
    ISBN 0-8167-0055-9 (lib. bdg.)
    ISBN 0-8167-4891-8 (pbk.)